CHICKEN SOUP for LITTLE SOULS READER

W9-AKV-634

The Best Night Out With Dad

Story Adaptation by
Lisa McCourt

Illustrated by
Bert Dodson

Story Adapted from "The Circus" by Dan Clark

SCHOLASTIC INC.

New York Toronto London Auckland Sydney
Mexico City New Delhi Hong Kong Buenos Aires

*For Mike McCourt, a dad who knows how to
make best nights.*
—L.M.

For Sydney, Riley, and Emily.
—B.D.

*In memory of S. Wayne Clark.
"Any male can be a father, but it takes a special man to be a dad."
I miss you, Dad.*
—D.C.

ISBN 0-439-69366-7

12 11 10 9 8 7 6 5 4 3 2   5 6 7 8 9 10/0

Printed in the U.S.A.   08

First printing, January 2005

CONTENTS

CHAPTER 1
"ROAR!"

"Roar!" Danny's father leaped out from behind the sofa. He pretended that his hands had giant claws. He roared like a tiger.

"Dad," said Danny, "stop being such a goofball."

"I'm not Dad!" Danny's father roared. "I'm Thor, king of the circus beasts!" He growled his scariest growl at Danny.

"I know you're excited about the circus, Dad," said Danny. "But you look more like a crazed gorilla than Thor."

"No gorillas at the circus," said Danny's father. "But I could be a dancing elephant. What do you think?" He did a clumsy ballet twirl.

"I think you need to stop being so silly," said Danny.

He smiled. He actually thought his dad was pretty funny.

But Danny felt too old to play pretend. He and his dad had been doing that forever. They always did it the night before they went to the circus.

"I'll call Coach tomorrow," said Danny's
father. "I'll tell him why you won't be at practice."

"Can't I go to practice first?" asked Danny.
He hated to skip a basketball practice. A big
game was coming up.

"I'm afraid there won't be time," said
Danny's father. "Remember how long the line
to buy tickets can be? Last year we almost
missed the opening act."

"Oh, yeah," said Danny. "And I don't want to miss that!" He put his arms up in the air like a real ringmaster. In his deepest, loudest voice, he said, "Welcome, ladies and gentlemen and children of all ages . . ."

"How come you still get to be the ringmaster and I can't be Thor anymore?" Danny's dad teased.

Danny went to his room to get ready for bed. He couldn't wait to see the circus again. It was his favorite thing to do with his dad. He looked up at the circus posters all over his walls. He closed his eyes and pretended he was there.

Danny loved everything about the circus. The

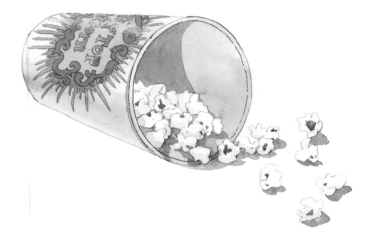

smell of the popcorn. He loved the music.
He loved the silly clowns and the thrilling acts.
He was so excited!

   Just one more day, and he'd be sitting right
there, in the front row, at his favorite place
on earth.

CHAPTER 2
Vincent

"Good thing we got here early!" Danny said to his father. The line to buy tickets was long. It stretched all the way around the big tent.

Danny felt the thrill of the circus all around him.

"Have you seen it?" asked a boy behind Danny in the line.

The boy pointed to Danny's sweatshirt. Danny's dad had bought it for him the last time

they went to the circus. It was his favorite
sweatshirt. It had a big picture of Thor,
the famous circus tiger, on it.

"A bunch of times," said Danny. "Haven't
you?"

The boy reached for his dad's hand. He
looked down. He shook his head no.

Right away, Danny was sorry he'd said it like that. The boy's clothes were kind of old looking. There was a hole in one of the elbows of his sweatshirt. His sneakers were almost worn through. Maybe this is the first time his family had enough money for the circus, Danny thought.

"What's your name?" Danny asked him.

"Vincent," said the boy, smiling again.

"Oh, boy, Vincent. Get ready for the best night of your life!" said Danny.

Vincent hopped up and down.

"How about if I tell you a thing or two about the circus? Then you will know what to expect," said Danny in a big-brother kind of way.

The smile on Vincent's face got even bigger. "Tell me," said Vincent. "Tell me everything!"

"Okay," said Danny.

"The circus has every cool thing you can think of. First you smell the popcorn. Then the big band starts to play. The ringmaster comes out in his shiny red coat and top hat. In a loud voice he says, 'Welcome, ladies and gentlemen and children of all ages . . .'"

"Why does he say that?" Vincent asked.

"Because everyone loves to come to the circus," said Danny. "So he wants to welcome everyone."

"Oh," said Vincent. "Okay."

Danny went on. "Acrobats come tumbling out in their sparkly costumes."

"Acro-whats?" asked Vincent.

"You're serious? You don't know what an acrobat is?"

Vincent shook his head.

"Okay," said Danny. "It looks like I'm going to have a lot to explain. Lucky for you, it's a long line.

"The acrobats do all those circus tricks. They jump and leap! They turn somersaults and cartwheels! They spin hoops on their arms and legs! They juggle rings and balls in the air!"

"I can do a somersault," said Vincent.

"Right. Okay. That's great," said Danny.
He rolled his eyes. But he was actually having
a good time with Vincent. It was fun telling
him everything about the circus.

17

CHAPTER 3
Horses, Dogs, and Clowns

Vincent just couldn't seem to hear enough about the circus. And Danny could talk forever about his favorite subject.

"What happens next? What happens next?" Vincent asked.

"Let's see. Oh, yeah, the horses. The horses come next," said Danny.

"The music gets kind of slow and spooky. The tent gets dark. All of a sudden, two white horses charge out of the darkness! They stand up on their hind legs. They dance around their trainer!"

Vincent's mouth dropped open. Danny tried not to laugh.

"Then the lights go up," said Danny.

"And the music gets faster. The horses gallop really fast around the ring. They jump through hoops that get higher and higher! More horses come out, with riders on them. The riders do flips off one horse and land on another!"

"No way!" shouted Vincent.

"Way," said Danny. "Don't ask me how they do it."

"What happens next?" Vincent wanted to know.

"The lights get low again. The music changes. The spotlight moves up, up, up to the high wire! A woman tiptoes across."

"What else does she do?" asked Vincent.

"She stands on one leg. She does a split on the wire! Then a man walks out onto the wire, too. He jumps and leaps. He does a backward somers—"

"Does he ever fall off?" Vincent interrupted.

"Oh, sure. That's what makes the circus so dangerous. And exciting."

Vincent bit his lip.

Danny said, "I'm just kidding you, buddy. They almost never fall off. They're real pros."

Danny bent down really close to Vincent. "I'll tell you a secret," he said. "There's a net just in case."

Vincent let out a big breath.

"What else? What else?" he begged.

"Let's see. There are the dogs! Yeah, the dogs do some really cool tricks."

"I have a dog," said Vincent. "His name is Rufus."

"Cool," said Danny. "But can your dog jump through a hoop?"

"Nope," said Vincent.

"Or bounce on a seesaw?"

"I don't think so," said Vincent.

"Well, the dogs at the circus can! And they can do more tricks than that. They're so funny! The big poodle pushes the little poodle around in a baby carriage. That's my favorite part of the dog act."

"I can't wait to see that!" said Vincent. "What comes next?"

"The clowns! The clowns are awesome! Some walk on stilts. They look about as tall as a house. Others ride super-high unicycles. Or drive wacky little cars!"

"Do they throw pies at each other?" asked Vincent.

"How did you know about that?"

"I saw it on T.V. once."

"Yeah, that's the best part! I love it when they throw pies. Sometimes they pretend to throw pies at people in the audience. I would love to get a pie in the face. Wham!"

"Yeah, wham!" shouted Vincent.

CHAPTER 4
Acrobats and Bears in Tutus

"Okay, what else?" said Danny.

"Oh, yeah, more acrobats. A couple of them hang from rings high up near the ceiling. They twist their bodies up like pretzels. Then they spin really fast.

"On the ground, two more acrobats hold on to each other's arms. Then they toss their brother up into the air. He does a double somersault and lands back in their arms.

"They throw him up again. He lands right on top of his brother's shoulders!" Danny continued.

"And wait till you see the bears in their tutus! The dancing bears will crack you up! Some of them ride motorcycles and even do wheelies. . . ."

"Dancing bears? No way!" said Vincent.

"You'd better believe me, because you're about to see them," said Danny.

"What about the elephants?!" asked Vincent.

He was so excited, he could barely get the words out.

"What do the elephants do?"

"Well, they dance, for one thing! They stand up on their hind legs. Sometimes they carry people around in their mouths. The coolest part is when an elephant holds a girl by his trunk and spins her around super fast.

"And the trapeze artists! They really fly! One swings across on a trapeze, then lets go. Another one catches her legs and swings her upside down. Then he lets go and she does a somersault in midair! At the end, one guy does a triple somersault blindfolded!"

Vincent's eyes were big and round.

"This is gonna be the best birthday present I ever got!" he yelled.

CHAPTER 5
Tickets

Danny's father bought their tickets. He said, "Ready, sport?"

"Wait, Dad," said Danny.

Then, to Vincent, he said, "But that's not even the best. The best, the very coolest act in the circus is THOR!" Danny pointed to his shirt. "Wait till you see this giant cat in action!"

Vincent hopped up and down. He was so excited. His dad stepped up to the window.

The ticket agent shook her head. "I'm sorry, sir. We don't accept this coupon anymore. You'll have to pay full price."

Vincent's father stood still.

In a small voice, Vincent said, "What's the matter, Dad? Aren't you going to buy the tickets?"

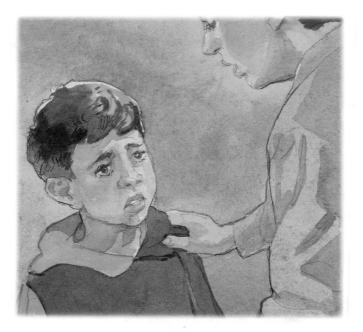

He doesn't have the money, Danny thought. His heart sank.

Vincent's father closed his wallet and gently pulled Vincent out of the line.

Vincent wouldn't see the circus. All of Danny's happiness melted away. He felt like crying.

He looked up at his dad and whispered, "What can we do?"

Danny's father thought for a moment.

Then he said, "You know, the basketball courts are open late tonight, son. Would you rather see the same old circus again or shoot some hoops instead?"

He handed Danny the two tickets he had just bought.

"It's up to you."

Danny understood right away. He thought about the decision his dad was letting him make.

A warm, good feeling filled Danny up inside. He smiled.

"I guess I could use the practice for Saturday's game. Let's go shoot some hoops!" he said.

Vincent and his father were already walking away.

"Hey, Vincent," Danny called. He ran to catch them.

Vincent turned around, wiping his nose on his sleeve.

"What?" he mumbled.

Danny saw the tear streaks on Vincent's face. For a moment, he didn't know what to say.

"I really liked telling you about the circus. And now I really want you to see it. I've got a basketball game this weekend. My dad and I are going to go practice. So it turns out we can't use these tickets after all." Danny held the tickets out to Vincent.

Vincent's face lit up. "Can we, Dad?"

Vincent's father looked at Danny with eyes full of thanks. Danny pressed the circus tickets into Vincent's hand. Then he ran back to his own dad.

Now it was Danny who wouldn't get to see the circus. But somehow, that didn't make him feel sad at all. Somehow, it made him feel really, really good.

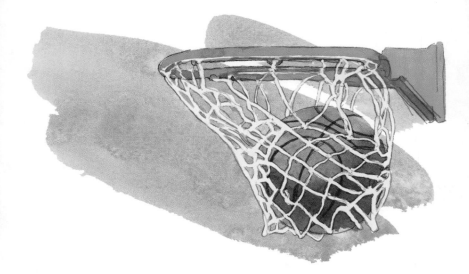

CHAPTER 6
The Very Best Night

On the basketball court, Danny was awesome. He had never made so many layups before! The cool night air filled his lungs. He was sweaty and tired, but he never wanted to stop playing.

Danny's dad was tired, too. "Want to go get a burger?" he asked Danny.

"Wait, Dad," said Danny. "I haven't done any free throws yet."

Danny's father passed him the ball. Danny stood on the line and got ready to throw. Before the ball even left his hands, he knew it was going in.

Swish!

Again.

Swish!

And again. And again. Danny made ten free throws in a row! That was the best anyone on his team had ever done!

He felt like he could have made twenty. But after ten baskets, Danny didn't want to push his luck.

He smiled at his dad. "I'm ready for that burger now," he said.

They usually went to the diner for burgers. But instead, Danny's father drove all the way to Burger Heaven. Burger Heaven had the best hamburgers and giant milk shakes.

The double-bacon cheeseburger Danny ate had never tasted better. Even his milk shake seemed extra-frosty and extra-chocolatey. Danny was so hungry, he even gobbled down a large order of fries.

Danny and his father walked back to their car. But before Danny could get in, his dad knelt down and hugged him hard.

"You did a very kind and special thing tonight, Danny," he said. "I'm so proud of you."

They didn't see the circus.

But to Danny, it was the best night out with Dad, ever.